WINTER
Wonderland

Illustrated by Alison Edgson

STRIPES PUBLISHING
An imprint the Little Tiger Group
1 Coda Studios, 189 Munster Road, London SW6 6AW

A paperback original
First published in Great Britain in 2014

ISBN: 978-1-84715-460-6

WINTER
Wonderland

stripes

CONTENTS

THE WINTER PARTY

Liss Norton

When Briar woke up, Mother Bear was sweeping the floor of the den. He sprang out of bed, instantly wide awake. "Today's the day, isn't it?" he whooped, fluffing his golden-brown fur with his front paws so that it stood up in spikes.

"Yes," said Mother Bear, smiling. "The Winter Party."

Briar ran over to hug her. "I can't wait!" he exclaimed, his feet jiggling impatiently as she smoothed the fur round his ears.

It would be his first *ever* Winter Party.

His friends had been talking about the party for weeks. It took place every year on the night before hibernation began, and there'd be twinkling lanterns and heaps of wonderful food. All the animals for miles around would be there, dancing, singing and making merry until dawn.

Mother Bear cooked some wild-oat porridge and they sat down to eat it. The fire was blazing and the den felt cosy, but Briar could hear the wind whistling outside.

"It's a north wind," Mother Bear told him. "There'll be snow later, for sure."

The bear cub felt a thrill of excitement. He'd never seen snow, but he'd heard all about how beautiful it was, covering everything with a thick layer of glistening whiteness.

"I'm getting the den ready for our long winter sleep," said Mother Bear, when breakfast was over. "And I want you to find food for the Winter Party, Briar."

"What sort of food?"

"Anything you can find," replied Mother Bear. "Berries, nuts or rose hips, fish or wild carrots." She handed him the gathering basket and he pulled on his woolly hat and scarf, then went out into the cold.

It was a clear, bright morning. Frost shimmered on the grass and he could see icicles glittering in the trees up ahead.

"I'll dig some wild carrots," Briar said to himself, licking his lips.

He scampered to the corner of the meadow where the wild carrots grew. The cold had turned their white flowers brown but he knew their roots would still be sweet and juicy. Putting down the basket, he began to dig, but the frost had made the ground as hard as stone and his claws couldn't break it.

"Never mind," he said. "I'll pick berries instead." He ran to the woods where an enormous holly tree grew.

The red holly berries shone like jewels and Briar climbed the tree eagerly, taking care not to brush against the prickly leaves. He soon filled his basket and slithered down again. He could help Mother Bear make a berry crumble for the party. Everyone would love that!

When he reached the ground, he heard wings clapping above his head. A huge flock of starlings flew down.

"Hello, Briar," they chirped. "Thanks for leaving some berries for us."

"Lucky I finished gathering mine before you came," giggled Briar, as they tucked in. There were so many starlings he was certain they'd pick the tree clean.

Sure enough, the berries were gone in no time at all and the starlings flew away again. "See you at the Winter Party!" they called.

Briar was about to set off for home when

he heard a gasp in the long grass at his feet.

"Oh no!" a shrill little voice wailed.

Briar bent down to see who was there. Millie, a tiny brown wood mouse, was peeping out of her home in the tree's roots.

"What's wrong?" asked Briar.

"The berries have all gone!" The little mouse's whiskers twitched miserably, then she began to cry. "I was planning to fill my cupboard with berries to feed my children through the winter," she sobbed. "But there aren't any left."

"Don't worry," said Briar kindly. "You can have mine." He tipped over his basket and the holly berries poured out.

Millie blinked away her tears. "Are you sure, Briar? Don't you need them for the Winter Party?"

"I can easily find something else," Briar told her. He helped her roll the berries in through her front door, glad to think that she'd have a full cupboard again and that her children wouldn't go hungry.

"Thank you," Millie said. "This food will last us all winter long." As she spoke a white feather drifted down.

Briar caught it on his paw, but it melted away to nothing. "That's funny," he said. "That feather vanished." He spotted another and another and looked up in surprise. Hundreds, perhaps thousands, of feathers were floating down between the trees' branches.

"They're snowflakes, not feathers," explained Millie. She shivered. "I'm going indoors to get warm. Thanks again."

"See you at the party," said Briar. Excitedly he watched the snowflakes drifting down. They were starting to settle on the ground, and on the twigs and brambles around him. He could have gazed at them all day long.

"But I've got to find food," he said. He set off through the woods, hoping to spot some tasty mushrooms or a few rose hips.

The woods were bare. There were no mushrooms or rose hips to be found, and no hazelnuts or crab apples, either. Briar sped up. He was starting to feel worried.

If he couldn't find food, he and Mother Bear might not be able to go to the Winter Party... He'd been looking forward to it for so long!

"Fish," he said, determined not to give up. "We can cook fish for the party." He ran out of the woods and back across the meadow. The snow was quite deep here and it flew up in a powdery, white shower with every step he took.

Soon he reached the river. Mother Bear had just started teaching him to fish and he hoped he could remember how to do it. He balanced on a large, flat stone near the water's edge, just as she'd shown him.

Peering into the water, he spotted a few fish, but they were so deep down that they were out of reach. "Perhaps the water's warmer down there," he sighed.

Briar watched and waited, but the fish didn't come to the surface. "It's no good," he said at last. "I'll have to go home and tell Mother Bear that I couldn't find anything to eat."

He shook off the snow that had settled on his fur, then trudged sadly away from the river. Suddenly he heard a cry: "Help!"

Briar dashed towards the sound and found Ruby Rabbit and her brothers and sisters sitting on a log surrounded by deep snow. "We're stuck, Briar!" Ruby said. "The snow's too deep. Can you please help us get home?"

Gently Briar picked up the smallest rabbits and popped them into his basket. "You older ones, climb up on my shoulders," he said.

Ruby helped her brothers and sisters scramble on, then she sprang up beside them. They all held on tightly to Briar's soft fur.

"Here we go then," he said. He hurried to the rabbits' home, a cosy burrow in a bank on the far side of the meadow.

"Thanks, Briar," chorused the little rabbits, as he stopped outside their front door. They slid down from his back and helped their tiny brothers and sisters out of his basket.

"My pleasure," said Briar.

Mrs Rabbit came out to welcome them home. "We'll have to get the sledge out tonight so we can get to the Winter Party," she said, as she looked up at the snowy sky. "Are you looking forward to it, Briar?"

"I don't think I'll be going," Briar replied sadly.

"Not going?" said Mrs Rabbit in astonishment. "Why ever not?"

Briar told her about his search for food. "I've looked everywhere," he said. "But it wouldn't be fair to go to the party without taking something to share."

"Wait right there," said Mrs Rabbit. She disappeared into her burrow, with all the little rabbits skipping after her.

When they came back, they were carrying an enormous cherry pie. "I baked two of these for the party," Mrs Rabbit said. "And I want you to have one as a reward for bringing my children home safely."

Briar gazed at the pie in delight. "Really?" he gasped. "For me?"

"Of course," said Mrs Rabbit. "You deserve it."

Briar put the pie carefully into his basket. "I'll see you all later," he called happily, as he headed for home.

The moon was high and the stars were twinkling in the black, velvety sky when Mother Bear and Briar set out for the party. It had stopped snowing, but the meadow was a blanket of silvery-white. Their paws made no sound as they crossed it, and the lantern Mother Bear carried threw sparkles of brightness all around.

As they drew closer to the wood, they saw all their friends heading in the same direction. Ruby and her rabbit brothers and sisters were riding on a sledge pulled by their father. Herbie Hedgehog and his family were wrapped up in so many coats and shawls that their prickles were completely hidden. And Millie Mouse and her children were riding on the back of Rosie Reindeer, whose antlers were decked with mistletoe.

"Hello, everyone," Briar called brightly.

"Hello, Briar," his friends called back, waving at him.

At last they reached the wood and hurried between the trees until they came to the wide clearing in the middle.

"Oh!" gasped Briar as he gazed around. "It's a winter wonderland!" Every tree was hung with flickering lanterns that set the snow glittering pink and blue and gold. Sparkling ice-crystal decorations covered the bushes, and log tables were piled high with cakes, tarts, biscuits and jugs of apple juice.

"Welcome to the Winter Party!" cried Bo Beaver. He signalled to the beaver band, who were waiting on a low stage. At once they began to play a cheerful tune, slapping their tails on the planks to keep time.

Briar found that his feet couldn't keep still. He stepped on to the dance floor and began whirling and skipping with his friends.

"I love parties!" he cried, as he twirled past Mother Bear.

"Me, too," she said, smiling.

The party ended at last. Briar held Mother Bear's paw as they headed for home. He was so happy he couldn't stop smiling, and his tummy was comfortably full of delicious food.

"The den's all ready for our hibernation," said Mother Bear. "We'll go straight to bed when we get home."

"And we'll stay asleep until the warm weather comes, won't we?" Briar asked.

"Yes," replied Mother Bear.

Briar yawned widely, feeling suddenly tired. "After that lovely party," he said, snuggling against Mother Bear, "we're going to have very sweet dreams."

WHO IS CHRISTMAS?

Anna Wilson

Henry was having a lovely dream. A kind stranger dressed in red and white was giving him a bowl full of oats and saying, "You have been a very good guinea pig this year."

Henry smiled and turned over in his comfy sawdust bed.

"Thank you," he said to the stranger. "Oats are my favourite. By the way, what is your name?"

"Henry."

"How funny," said Henry. "That's my name, too."

"HENRY!"

"Eh? What—?"

"HENRY, WAKE UP!"

The guinea pig blinked and shuffled out of his warm nest with an irritable squeak. "What is it? I was having a lovely dream. Oh, it's you," he said, coming face to face with the white kitten, Scoot. "Why are you bothering me again?"

"I'm not bothering you," Scoot protested. "I have some extremely important news."

"Oh yes?" said Henry, yawning.

Scoot was always rushing to Henry with important news that mainly turned out to be not important at all, and often not even news for that matter.

"It's about Indoors…" said Scoot. He paused dramatically and then said, "Christmas is coming!"

"Who is Christmas?" asked Henry.

"I don't know," Scoot admitted. "But everything Indoors has been turned topsy-turvy and the Big Ones and Little Ones are being weird."

Henry tutted. "You are being ridiculous."

"The Big Ones have brought a TREE Indoors!" Scoot announced.

Henry laughed. "Trees are much too big to go Indoors, everyone knows that."

"Well, they have," said Scoot. "I wish you lived Indoors, then you could see for yourself."

At that exact moment, Henry's hutch was lifted high into the air, which made

Henry do a backwards somersault. His head ended up in his food bowl.

"What have you done, Scoot?" he squeaked. "Didn't anyone ever tell you to be careful what you wish for?"

But Scoot was already out of earshot as Henry and his hutch went on a bumpy, noisy ride. He felt quite travel-sick. Above him, Henry heard some voices that he recognized as belonging to the Big Ones.

"I hope Henry won't mind."

"It's for the best. If it snows, he'll be far too cold outdoors."

Suddenly, Henry's hutch was set down with a bump.

"Henry? Henry!"

It was Scoot.

"WHAT?" Henry squeaked, as he

shuffled to the wire mesh of his front door.

"Have you seen the tree?" Scoot mewed.
"They've covered it in shiny things. Look!"
The little cat gestured with his paw.

He was right. There before them was
a large green tree, covered
in sparkly lights, silver
balls and lengths of
shiny, bristly
silver stuff.

"What is going on?" Henry whispered.

But Scoot didn't get a chance to reply.

"You naughty thing," said one of the Big Ones, "playing with the decorations! Christmas only comes to good little kittens! I'm putting you next door, out of the way..."

Scoot protested loudly, "Meeeeooooow!", and then he was gone.

Poor Scoot! Henry thought, horrified. *I must try and find out who this Christmas is. But how on earth can I while I'm shut in here? I have to get out. I wish someone would open the door...*

No sooner had Henry thought this, than a small, chubby hand opened the hutch and reached inside. "Christmas is coming, Henry! It's so exciting!"

Henry saw his chance and grabbed it. He made a rush for the exit and, in a panic, ran to the sparkly tree, thinking that it looked like the best place to hide. Once he was safely behind the wide trunk, he squashed himself against it, his heart beating wildly.

Footsteps pattered out of the room, accompanied by a faint wailing. "Henry's goooooooonnnnne!"

I had better make the most of my freedom while I can, he told himself.

He crept out, checking carefully around to make sure no one was about to grab him.

"Hello! Hello!" shouted someone from above.

Henry peered up.

"Hello! Hello!" The voice came from a colourful bird in a cage on a stand.

"Oh goodness, you scared me!" said Henry. "Hello, I'm Henry. Who are you?"

"Christmas is coming! Christmas is coming!" rasped the bird.

At this, Henry pricked up his tiny ears. "Aha!" he said. "What do you know about Christmas?"

"Christmas is coming! Christmas is—"

"Yes, yes," said Henry. "Feather-brain," he muttered.

He turned back to the tree and came face to face with a pair of huge slobbery jaws full of terrifyingly pointy teeth.

"Eeeeeek!" squealed Henry. "It's you – the dog! I didn't know you lived Indoors."

"And I thought you lived Outdoors,"

said the dog. He licked his enormous white teeth and asked, "Are you on the menu for lunch today? A tasty starter, perhaps?"

"I am nobody's lunch, thank you very much!" cried Henry. "I-I'm here to try and find out who Christmas is. Can you tell me?" He thought that if he kept the dog talking, he might get away without being eaten.

"Errrr, I'm not sure," said the dog. "I do know that I get a lovely lunch when Christmas comes, though. Delicious sausages and bacon and bits of turkey all covered with gravy…"

The dog seemed to go into a trance: he began swaying. "Mmmm! Sausages … bacon … turkey."

"Very interesting," said Henry. "But who is Christmas?"

"Sausages … bacon … turkey…"

CRASH!

One of the silver baubles fell from the tree and smashed into pieces on the dog's head. The dog immediately started barking angrily and leaping at the decorations.

Henry scurried under the tree to hide and catch his breath.

All at once there was the sound of running and shouts of, "Oh! You naughty dog!"

"We'll have to keep him out."

"Put him in the kennel while Henry's on the loose."

"Psst!" came a voice from among the branches.

"What now?" groaned Henry, who was wishing he had stayed safely in his hutch.

The tree began to shake, then, with a thud, Scoot landed at Henry's feet. He was covered in prickly green needles and his tail was decorated with a trail of silver glittery stuff.

"How did you get back in here?" Henry gasped.

"Cats are good at escaping," said Scoot. "We are also good at spying," he added.

"Oh yes?" Henry said.

"Yes. I have discovered that the dog thinks you are on the menu for lunch today," Scoot whispered, his eyes wide.

"So I hear." Henry swallowed hard. "Anything else? About Christmas, I mean?"

"It's coming tonight!" Scoot hissed.

Henry shivered with excitement. "In that case, we should stay put and keep our eyes and ears open."

The house fell silent. The only light came from the tiny bulbs nestled in the greenery of the special Indoor tree. The guinea pig and the kitten curled up together under the sweet-smelling branches. They were just about to doze off when there was a scrabbling sound, followed by a bump and a fit of coughing.

Henry nudged Scoot and whispered, "Listen!"

"These chimneys are getting slimmer," said a low voice. "Or am I getting fatter? Ah! Mince pies. Diet begins tomorrow…"

Henry and Scoot crept out to get a closer look.

A large, kindly looking man dressed in red and white was helping himself to some food he had found on a table by the fireplace. Henry saw he had a sack slung over his shoulders and—

"It's — it's the person from my dream!" exclaimed Henry.

"What?" said Scoot.

The stranger turned and saw them. "What are you two doing up and about at this late hour?"

Henry froze, but Scoot bounded over and said, "Are you Christmas?"

"Christmas is not a person!" chortled the stranger.

"Oh," said Scoot, disappointed.

"But some people call me *Father* Christmas," said the man.

"Ah!" cried Scoot. Then he looked puzzled. "I don't understand."

Father Christmas bent down and tickled Scoot under his chin. "I come at Christmas time to make wishes and dreams come true."

With that, he reached deep into a pocket and brought out a toy mouse. "For you," he said. He threw it to Scoot, who began to play with the toy, tossing it in the air, and batting it to and fro with his tiny white paws.

"And these," he went on, setting a bowl down in front of Henry, "are for you."

He filled it to the brim with tasty oats and patted the guinea pig.

"Oh," breathed Henry.

"Now I must give the children their presents, leave a bone outside for the dog and drop some seeds into the parrot's cage. Happy Christmas!" The man winked and turned to go.

The next morning, Henry awoke in his hutch. "What a strange dream," he muttered, scurrying over to his bowl. He peered inside. "Oats! So, it wasn't a dream this time!" he cried.

He was about to tuck in when a Little One came bounding over and said, "Look – Henry's back in his hutch!"

A Big One bent down to look inside. "There you are," it said to the Little One. "I told you Father Christmas made wishes and dreams come true."

"How right you are," said Henry.

But of course, they did not hear him, for his mouth was full of oats.

THE BEST
BATH

Lucy Courtenay

Snow lay deep and white on the ground in the mountains of Japan. The trees of the forest stretched their icy branches into the low hanging clouds, disappearing like ghosts in the mist.

A troop of snow monkeys climbed down from the biggest tree in the forest, sniffing at the chilly air. Thirty, forty, fifty monkeys, all jumping off the lowest branches to land as silent as feathers in the snow.

The littlest monkey, Saru, clung tightly

to his mother Haha's back, gazing fearfully at the whiteness below. The forest looked so strange and new in its blanket of snow.

"Look at you, Saru," scoffed Saru's older brother, Ani, leaping past with a scornful flick of his short brown tail. "Still riding on Haha's back like a baby!"

"Stop teasing Saru, Ani," said their mother. "Don't forget that you once rode on my back, too."

Ani looked annoyed. "That was so long ago, it's hardly worth mentioning."

When they reached the smooth white snow at the foot of the tree, Saru jumped off his mother's back as quickly as he could. He landed in a deep patch and for a moment he panicked as he felt it freeze his paws and sink away beneath him.

"I'll carry you a little further, Saru," said Haha. "The snow here is too deep."

Saru's ears felt hot at the sound of Ani's scornful laughter, but he climbed on to his mother's back again. What choice did he have?

The snow monkeys walked together through the forest, huddled close for warmth. The air bit down as hard as a hungry lynx. Saru shivered and snuggled into the cosy long brown fur on his mother's back, secretly glad of the ride.

The snow monkeys walked a long way, through a part of the forest Saru didn't recognize. Ani and his friends scampered back and forth among the adults, laughing and rolling snowballs at each other. Saru wanted to join in, but he didn't dare.

Ani wouldn't let me join in anyway, he thought gloomily.

As the trees thinned, Saru saw a wide stretch of icy rocks before them. He slid off Haha's back on to a nearby rock and sniffed the air in surprise. It smelled strange. Hot and steamy, and a little bit rotten.

Blop. Blop, blop, blop.

51

"What's that noise?" Saru said, suddenly feeling anxious.

"The hot springs," his mother answered. "Look after Saru, won't you, Ani? I'll see you boys later."

Saru watched his mother and the other adult monkeys climb up and over the rocks and vanish from sight. A splashing sound made Saru jump.

"She probably won't come back, you know," said Ani.

Saru felt scared. He looked at the place where his mother had disappeared. "Why not?"

"Because of the monster!"

Ani grinned and scampered up the rocks after his friends. Saru followed, feeling more scared than ever.

"What monster?" he asked. "Ani? Ani!"

He stopped short at his first sight of the springs.

Two deep pools sat side by side, divided by a wide rocky ridge. The rotten smell was stronger than ever, and the water hissed and bubbled. *Blop. Blop. Blop.* All around, monkeys were bathing and playing and jumping into the hot water's steamy depths.

"What monster?" Saru repeated.

Ani was already floating in the water with his paws behind his head. "The monster who lives in these springs, of course. Can't you smell him?"

Saru sniffed the rotten air unhappily. Was it the smell of a monster?

Ani's eyes gleamed with amusement.

"Its eyes are as black as night. Its whiskers are long and pale, and its teeth are sharp and hungry. It lives under the water. Of course," he added, relaxing against the rocks, "it wouldn't dare to eat me. But it eats mother monkeys and baby monkeys all the time."

"I don't believe you," said Saru.

Ani grinned. "Then why aren't you getting in?"

None of the other monkeys looked scared of monsters. They looked like they were having lots of fun. Saru wished he could see Haha, but he couldn't.

I mustn't let Ani see that I'm scared, he thought.

"I'm coming in," he said loudly.

He shuffled closer to the edge of the steaming water. He looked down, just in case.

Two eyes as black as night stared back at him. Pointed teeth glinted at him.

Saru shrieked with terror and bounded away from the springs as fast as his little legs would carry him. Stumbling and falling in the snow, he ran and ran. Through trees, over rocks, under bushes and over branches. He imagined the monster's hot, rotten breath on his neck and its claws reaching out—

Saru fell head over heels into a snowdrift. He lay there trying to catch his breath, and gazed with frightened eyes at the strange white forest all around him. He'd never known it to be so quiet. Only the slipping sound of snow sliding off branches broke the stillness. Saru climbed out of the snowdrift, shivering all over.

He had never been all by himself before.

He tried not to feel scared.

Haha will find me, he told himself. *I just have to wait.*

He rolled some snowballs the way he

had seen Ani and his friends do. It was fun, especially when the snowballs got bigger. If only the snow wasn't so deep. It made his tummy feel wet and cold, even through his thick fur.

The misty white light in the forest was fading and still his mother hadn't come to find him. The tip of Saru's short tail started feeling numb. His toes tingled next. Then his fingers.

What would happen when the sun set? There were other predators in these mountains, besides the monster in the springs. Eagles and lynxes. They would snap him up for sure.

Saru curled into a miserable snowy ball at the foot of a tree, tucked his nose under his stumpy tail, and waited for the end to come.

"*Saru!* Where are you, you silly little baby?"

It was Ani.

Saru uncurled his stiff body and ran towards his big brother. He had never been so pleased to see him in his life.

"ANI!" he cried.

Ani pushed him away. "Haha told me off for scaring you," he said sulkily. "Why did you run away? That monster story was only a joke!"

Saru was confused. "But I saw it! It had eyes and teeth, just like you said!"

"That was *you*, silly," Ani grumbled. "Your reflection."

Saru felt more confused than ever. "What's a 'flection?"

"When you look in the springs, the light

shines on the top of the water and shows you what your own face looks like."

"I look like a monster?" said Saru.

"That's a matter of opinion," grunted Ani. "And now I'm in trouble just because my little brother can't take a joke!"

Saru was furious. "It wasn't a very funny joke!" he said.

Ani grinned. "I thought it was hilarious. Come on, or Haha will shout at me again."

Saru hopped and ran after his brother as best he could. He wanted to ride on Ani's back, but he knew his brother would push him off and call him a baby, so he struggled on through the thick snow, shivering all over.

The moon had risen behind the mountains now, striping the snow with black shadows and a clear, soft light. When they reached the springs, the water looked almost magical, swirling and steaming and reflecting the bright moon overhead. There were monkeys lying in the shining pools, their eyes closed and their bodies warm and relaxed.

Without a second glance, Ani leaped into the first pool to join his friends. Saru saw his mother in the deepest part of the pool, her head tipped to the stars. She looked round at the sound of Ani's splash. Saru waved, happy to see her. Haha waved back.

The little monkey looked carefully at the moonlit water by his feet. The same eyes gleamed at him as before. He opened his mouth, and his own teeth flashed at him.

Ani was right. The monster had been his reflection all along.

As Saru slid into the shallow pool, a wonderful feeling of warmth stole up his shivering little body. It spread through his blood like a forest fire. Saru's frozen muscles relaxed. The water only came up to his chin, so he dipped his head and felt the heat of the springs soothe his chilled face. It was wonderful. Magical. Not scary at all.

Saru had an idea.

He climbed out of the pool and hunted around the rocks, choosing the two biggest, blackest pebbles he could find. A fistful of sharp white stones was next. Last of all, Saru snapped off six slim twigs from a pine tree and stripped away their rough, dark bark with his teeth until the pale wood gleamed underneath.

He climbed back into the steaming water with his treasures, and started to build a picture on the bottom of the pool.

Two pebbly eyes as black as night.

Twiggy whiskers that were long and pale.

White stone teeth, sharp and hungry and curved into a snarl.

When he was happy with the result,

Saru lay back in the hot, hot water – and waited.

"Having fun?" Ani appeared near Saru, grinning.

"Lots of fun without you, thanks," said Saru.

Ani leaped into Saru's pool with a great splash. "Now, what game shall we play?" he said. "I know. How about 'dunk the baby brother'?"

He reached over to push Saru under the water but Saru dodged his paw.

"I'll get you next time," Ani laughed, settling down comfortably against the rocks.

The moon scudded out from behind a cloud. On the pool's rocky bottom, two pebbly black eyes, six long pale twiggy whiskers and a fistful of shiny stone teeth gleamed in a bright shaft of moonlight.

Saru pointed.

"Ani!" he shouted. "The monster's back. And it looks hungry!"

Ani's eyes bulged with shock at the sight of the big stony, twiggy face glaring up at him from the bottom of the pool.

"AAARGH!" Ani yelled in terror, leaping out of the water with a clumsy splash. "THERE'S A MONSTER! THERE'S A MONSTER IN THE SPRINGS! AAARGH!"

He sprinted away into the dark forest with his stumpy tail rammed tightly between his legs.

Haha put her head over the rocks.

"Is everything all right, Saru?" she said. "Is Ani teasing you again?"

Saru used his toes to scuff out the monster on the bottom of the pool, then smiled his biggest smile.

"Don't worry, Haha," he said. "I can take care of myself."

THE SILVER
REINDEER

Linda Chapman

Ellie kneeled on the floor of her bedroom and cantered her model pony over the jumps she had made out of some twigs from the garden. She let herself imagine she was riding a real pony. Just three jumps left, two jumps, one jump... "And that's a clear round for Ellie and Prince!" she declared.

She sat back and sighed, loneliness washing over her. It was Christmas Eve and all her friends at Elms Farm, the riding school she used to go to, would be having a big party. But Ellie and her parents had just moved house and Elms Farm was too far away. She didn't know anyone in Ashton, their new village. Christmas wasn't going to be much fun this year.

She wished she could go and talk to her mum and dad but they were round at their new neighbours' house for the evening. Maybe she should go and talk to Jenny, the babysitter? But when she'd gone downstairs before, Jenny had been talking on her phone and had waved her away.

Ellie went to the window. The lawn and trees were covered with a thick layer of snow. It was the perfect Christmas scene but Ellie didn't feel Christmassy at all. She looked up at the stars, twinkling high overhead.

"I wish I had some friends to play with tonight... I wish I wasn't so lonely," Ellie whispered.

One of the stars in the sky suddenly flashed brightly and then went out. Ellie blinked in surprise. She'd never seen a star do that before. Then a movement caught her eye. She looked down and gasped out loud. A silver reindeer with large antlers had appeared on the lawn!

Ellie stared. What was going on? There couldn't be a reindeer in her garden! She turned and ran down the stairs, pausing in the lounge doorway.

"Jenny…"

But Jenny was still talking on her phone.

Ellie hurried on into the kitchen. There were large French windows at the end of it that opened on to the garden. She put on her wellies and stepped outside, her heart beating fast.

The reindeer was still there, every hair on his body shining with a silvery light. His large dark eyes looked at her.

"Hello, Ellie," he said.

Ellie didn't see his lips move but she heard his voice in her head.

"Hello," she breathed, her heart pounding

in her chest as she walked over. This was magic – real magic! The reindeer nuzzled her hands, his breath warming her fingers.

"My name is Silver," he told her. "I come from Star World."

"Star World?" Ellie echoed.

Silver nodded. "It's a magical world. Every Christmas Eve we send wishing stars from our world into your sky. If a child wishes on one of those stars, their wish might just come true." He rubbed his head against her arm. "I'm here to grant your wish!"

If Ellie hadn't felt the cold biting into her cheeks and seen her breath freezing in clouds in the air, she would have thought she was dreaming. "What do you mean?"

Silver's dark eyes twinkled. "Get on my

back and you'll see!"

Ellie climbed on to his back and straightaway a tingly warmth flooded through her.

Silver tossed his antlers. "Hold on tight, Ellie! We're going on a starlight adventure!"

He leaped into the sky. Ellie gasped in alarm but then she realized she felt completely safe, like there was no way she could fall off Silver's back. He cantered higher and higher and then the world seemed to spin around in a blur of silver light. As it cleared, Ellie saw that her garden was no longer beneath them. Instead there was a snowy land with hills, trees, frozen lakes and little wooden houses dotted around. Every bit of it sparkled and twinkled as if it was coated in stardust.

"Welcome to Star World," Silver said.

He landed lightly on the snow. Four other silver reindeer cantered over from the forest. They surrounded Ellie, nuzzling her with their soft muzzles and blinking at her through long eyelashes.

"Hello, Ellie," said one who had darker silver dapples. "I'm Starshine. And these are

my friends: Merrylegs, Sparkle and Holly."
The reindeer who were being introduced
each nodded as their names were spoken.
They pushed their heads forward to be
stroked. Their fur was soft and thick. Ellie
had never seen such beautiful animals.

"You're going to have a wonderful time
with us, Ellie," said Starshine.

"But what about my babysitter and my
parents? They'll be worried when they
notice I've gone," Ellie realized.

"It's all right – time passes differently in
our world and yours," said Silver. "No one
will know you've been away."

"Come with us and meet the elves,"
said Holly, who had a patch of white fur
shaped like a holly leaf in the centre of her
forehead.

The reindeer all trotted into the forest with Ellie on Silver's back. Every so often Silver and the other reindeer would stop to point something out to Ellie – like the flock of tiny blue ice dragons they came across, flapping from branch to branch like little birds. The ice dragons circled round Ellie's head and perched on Silver's neck, showing her how they could blow streams of ice crystals out of their nostrils. Further on, Ellie met some fluffy mice who could roll themselves up to look like snowballs, and then a litter of friendly snow-fox cubs came to say hello to her. They could make rainbow sparks of light fly into the air like mini fireworks whenever they waved their bushy tails. It was all so magical!

Finally they arrived at a frozen lake.

There were people ice-skating on it.

No, not people, Ellie realized. People didn't have such large, pointed ears. They had to be elves!

Two elves came skating over, a boy and a girl.

"This is Ellie, she's from the human world," Silver said.

"Hi, Ellie." The girl smiled. "I'm Stella and this is my brother, Casper."

"Come skating with us, Ellie!" said Casper. He magicked a pair of sparkling skates out of the air and held them out to her.

Ellie climbed off Silver's back and put the skates on. Then she set off on the ice with Stella and Casper holding her hands. At home, she wasn't that great at ice-skating, but here she found her feet seemed to know just what to do and she didn't fall over once.

When they got tired of skating, Stella and Casper took Ellie over to a wooden hut. An older elf was serving up mugs of hot chocolate with marshmallows on top and iced star-shaped cookies.

After they had finished their biscuits and hot chocolate, Ellie, Stella and Casper each jumped on to a reindeer and played chase, flying through the starry sky. Ellie didn't think she'd ever had such fun, but at last she started to yawn.

"It's time to take you home," Silver said to her softly.

She nodded sleepily.

"Goodbye, Ellie!" all her new friends called. "Don't forget us!"

"Never," said Ellie, her eyes shining. "This has been the best night of my life. Goodbye!" She waved to them as Silver raced up into the sky.

She felt the same twirling, swirling sensation as starlight surrounded them. Then they were swooping down towards her garden.

Silver landed. "Thank you for granting my wish," she said, hugging him as she dismounted.

"It's not over yet," Silver said. "There's still another part to come."

"What do you mean?" Ellie asked.

Silver blew softly on her hair. "You'll find out in the morning. Happy Christmas, Ellie. Always remember – wishes really can come true."

And with that he leaped back into the sky. Ellie watched him go, not knowing whether to feel sad that her adventure was over or excited about what he had said. What did he mean?

She watched until he disappeared in a flash of silver and then she let herself back into the house and crept upstairs to her bedroom.

Ellie was so tired that as soon as she got into bed she fell fast asleep.

In the morning when Ellie woke up, her feet touched a pillowcase at the end of her bed and she heard the rustle of presents. Excitement whooshed through her. It was Christmas Day! She threw back the covers. "Mum! Dad!" she shouted. "It's Christmas!"

She had just started unwrapping her presents when her parents came into her room in their dressing gowns.

"Happy Christmas, sweetheart!" her mum said.

Ellie hugged them both. "Santa's been!"

"I can see," her dad said with a smile. "And there's also a very special present from us waiting for you outside."

Ellie frowned. Outside? What sort of present would be outside?

"Go to the window," her mum said, looking excited.

Ellie ran to the window and pulled open the curtains. A golden Palomino pony was standing in the garden! She stared in shock. "It's a ... a pony!"

Her dad came over and put his arm round her. "She's yours to look after, if you want."

Ellie couldn't believe it. "Yes! Of course I want to! But how? Why?"

"It all happened last night when we were at the Wilsons' house," her mum said. "It was so strange. We were at the party when I saw this pony appear at the window. At first I thought I was imagining things but it turned out she belongs to the Wilsons' daughter, Anna, and she'd broken out of her paddock."

"I told Mr Wilson how much you like horses," Ellie's dad said. "And he said that Anna is much too big for the pony now and they'd be more than happy if you wanted to ride her and look after her. Anna will show you what to do and she'll also take you up to the local riding school so you can make friends there."

"So, what do you think?" Ellie's mum said.

"Yes, please!" Ellie gasped. "What's she called?"

"Angel," her mum said. "Why don't you go and see her?"

Ellie raced downstairs and ran outside. Giving a friendly whicker, Angel came over to say hello, her dark eyes blinking at Ellie through her long white forelock.

Ellie wrapped her arms round Angel's neck and breathed in the sweet pony smell. "Oh, you're beautiful!" she said.

Angel nuzzled her.

"It's so strange that Angel appeared at the window like that last night," said her mum. "Almost like magic."

Ellie smiled. If only her mum knew! *Thank you, Silver,* she thought as she hugged her new pony tightly. *You were right. Wishes really can come true.*

A PRESENT FOR
MICKLEMOUSE

Katy Cannon

"Come on, Merry! We can't be late for Micklemouse!" Merry's big sister, Molly, carolled out, the words ringing down the tunnels and round the corners of their little maze-like home, tucked under the roots of the old oak tree.

Merry tugged on her jacket, which was woolly and lined with feather fluff for warmth. "I'm coming!" she called back.

She didn't want to be late to see Micklemouse any more than Molly did!

After all, if they missed him at the Frost Fair, how would he know what toys they wanted in their stockings this Christmas?

Outside the air was crisp and cold. Mama Mouse had hung a string of glistening raindrops from a cobweb above their little wooden door, and they'd frozen into icicles, shining like fairy lights in the winter sun.

"It's the perfect sort of day for a Frost Fair," Papa Mouse announced, crunching over the frozen leaves towards them. "They say the stream is iced over all the way to the edge of the woods. Micklemouse will have no problem getting his sleigh down there today!"

"I'm going to tell him that I want an acorn tea set for my toys," Molly announced.

"I want a proper wooden train set,

with carriages and everything," their brother, Matty, said.

"What about you, Merry?" Papa Mouse asked. "What are you going to ask Micklemouse for this year?"

Merry frowned. "I'm not sure."

Papa Mouse wrapped an arm round her shoulders. "Don't worry. You'll think of something on the way there. Or maybe Micklemouse will have some ideas!"

Papa Mouse was right. Micklemouse was the perfect person to ask. He made all the toys, so he'd know which one she'd like.

But then Merry had a thought. If Micklemouse gave toys and presents to all the mice, who gave Micklemouse *his* present?

Merry kept wondering about this as the family set off from the old oak tree towards the stream, meeting several other families of mice on their way. Some of them were old friends who lived nearby. Others had travelled much further and were mice Merry and her family only ever saw on Frost Fair day. All of them were in high spirits, and there was plenty of singing and laughter as they marched along the side of the stream.

But Merry kept frowning.

"What's up, baby mouse?" Papa Mouse asked, using his pet name for her. "It's the Frost Fair! There's no time for frowns today."

"I was just wondering about something," Merry explained.

"What were you wondering, Merry?" Papa Mouse gave her a smile. "Maybe I can help."

"Who gives Micklemouse his Christmas present?" Merry looked up at Papa Mouse and waited for an answer. Papa Mouse always knew the answer to everything.

But Papa Mouse's whiskers drooped. "Do you know, Merry, I'm not sure. But someone must. After all, everyone gets a present at Christmas!"

For the rest of the journey, Merry and

Papa Mouse asked everyone they met the same question. But nobody seemed to know the answer. Nobody even seemed to have thought about it before!

By the time the bunting and stalls of the Frost Fair came into sight, and just as they heard the first Christmas carols, Merry had really started to worry.

What if no one gave Micklemouse a Christmas present *at all*?

The Frost Fair sparkled with snowflakes and candlelight, and the crisp, cold air smelled of hot sweet apple drinks and gingerbread. Merry hurried along behind her family, past wooden stalls selling gifts and treats and past the mice ice-skating on the frozen pond. Afterwards, they'd have time to explore the whole fair. But first, it was time to see Micklemouse!

Micklemouse's grotto was set into the roots of a very old tree, right in the centre of the Frost Fair. Leading away from the tree was a long queue of mice, all wrapped up in scarves and jackets, just like Merry and her family. When the mice spoke, she could see their breath appear as white puffs in the wintry air.

"I'm sure we won't have to wait too long," Mama Mouse said, huddling close to Papa Mouse.

"It'll be worth it anyway," Matty said.

"And afterwards we can go skating!" Molly added.

As they waited, one of Micklemouse's assistants came down the line, handing out bowls of acorn stew.

"Do you know what you're going to ask for this year, little mouse?" Micklemouse's assistant asked Merry.

Merry shook her head. "I'm not sure yet. But…" she hesitated. Surely, if anyone knew the answer to her question, it would be Micklemouse's helper. "I was wondering. Do you know who gives Micklemouse his Christmas present?"

The assistant's eyes widened in surprise.

"Well … you see… Do you know, I don't think Micklemouse actually gets a Christmas present."

Merry gasped. "But why not?"

"He's always so busy – making the toys and presents. And we all help him get ready. Then, after he flies off on Christmas Eve to deliver them, we assistants go home to our families for Christmas dinner, and he… Well, I think by the time he gets home he's so tired he just goes to bed."

"But that's … that's terrible!" Merry whispered.

Micklemouse's assistant patted her on the head. "Don't worry about Micklemouse, little mouse. Giving presents to other people is what makes him happiest. He has the best job in the world," she said, moving on to the next family in the queue.

But Merry *did* worry. Poor Micklemouse. No presents. No Christmas dinner. No family around him on Christmas Day. And after he spent Christmas Eve delivering toys and presents to all the other mice! It just wasn't fair.

So Merry decided she would do something about it.

Checking to make sure no one was watching, Merry sneaked away from the queue. Her parents were chatting with the people ahead of them, and Molly and Matty were bickering about the best toy to ask Micklemouse for. No one would notice as long as she wasn't gone too long. All she needed was enough time to buy Micklemouse a present, then she'd sneak back.

It would take no time at all.

But once she was out among the stalls of the Frost Fair again, it didn't seem so simple. Everything looked bigger without Papa Mouse beside her, and nowhere had quite the right present for Micklemouse.

She tried the stall with ribbons and bows hanging from strings, but she didn't think Micklemouse was the sort for ribbons. She found one stall selling all sorts of wonderful toys – but they weren't quite as special as the ones Micklemouse made himself.

One stall was too expensive, one too crowded for Merry to even get near. One had a counter too tall for Merry to look over, and the last stall she tried was already closing up, its goods packed away in boxes.

Watching the sun sink down over

the frozen stream, Merry realized she'd been gone far longer than she'd meant to. Mama Mouse and Papa Mouse would be worrying, her feet were aching from walking so far in one day, and it had all been for nothing. She still didn't have a present for Micklemouse.

Whiskers drooping and heart heavy, Merry was about to start trudging back towards Micklemouse's tree when suddenly a white-gloved paw landed on her shoulder.

Merry jumped, her eyes widening, but when she turned, she saw the kind face of Micklemouse himself, looking down at her!

"Where have you been, Merry?" Micklemouse asked. "I've been looking everywhere for you. You're the only mouse not to come and see me today, and I have a very special present for you."

"I'm so sorry!" Merry cried. "But it was important! I needed to, well, you see … I wanted *you* to have a present this Christmas, too."

Micklemouse smiled. "Come, Merry. Let's go and find your family."

Mama Mouse and Papa Mouse were very happy to see that Merry was safe, and Mama Mouse gave her a big hug.

"What have we said about wandering off alone?" she scolded, holding Merry at arm's length and looking straight into her eyes.

Merry scuffed a foot against the floor. "Never ever to do it. I'm sorry. I won't ever do it again."

"I'm very glad to hear that," Micklemouse

said. "But I believe that Merry had only the best of intentions. And I would still like to give her a special present."

Merry looked up hopefully as Micklemouse reached into his sack, pulling out a sparkling glass ball on top of a golden stand.

"Thank you!" Merry took the present and studied it closely. Inside the glass ball stood a little figure of Micklemouse himself, with his arm round another tiny mouse – a mouse who looked just like Merry! When Merry shook the globe, tiny flakes of snow came falling down on to the figures.

She beamed. "I love it!"

"Happy Christmas to you, Merry," Micklemouse said.

Merry threw her arms round him and gave him a great big hug. "I still don't have anything to give you."

"That's all right, Merry," Micklemouse said. "My gift, every Christmas, is to see the joy and pleasure I can bring by giving to others, and making little mice happy. That is a very great gift indeed." Then he winked. "But a thank-you card is always nice!"

Merry nodded. She supposed that it was always fun to give presents, as well as to get them.

"And now it's time to go home," Papa Mouse said. "Thank you again, Micklemouse, for finding our Merry."

They all chorused their thanks and goodbyes, and Merry followed her family back out into the snow. It was time to head home for their Christmas Eve sleep, ready for the big day tomorrow.

Merry grinned with excitement. There would be food and presents, family and singing and fun. She couldn't wait!

But then, she turned back and saw Micklemouse climbing on to his sleigh, all alone on Christmas Eve. Despite everything he'd said, she wished that she could give him a proper Christmas, too.

Suddenly, Merry gasped. She could! She might not have a gift for Micklemouse this Christmas, but she did have something that she could *share*. Something she thought Micklemouse would enjoy very much indeed.

Breaking away from Mama Mouse and
Papa Mouse, she dashed over to the sleigh.

"Micklemouse? When you've delivered
all the presents, would you like to come to
our home for Christmas dinner? There'll be
singing and decorations and everything!"

She glanced back at Mama Mouse and Papa Mouse. They were both nodding and smiling.

"It would be an honour to have you," Mama Mouse said.

A broad smile broke out across Micklemouse's face. "Thank you, Merry," he said. "To share in your Christmas would be the very best present of all."

PAWPRINTS IN THE SNOW

Holly Webb

"Just *look* at it!" Sophie whispered. Her breath settled on the freezing window glass in a wisp of mist.

"Is it sticking? Is it going to stay?" Jake wriggled up next to her, squeezing on to the deep windowsill and peering out at the crazy whirl of snowflakes.

There was a thin, cold draught slicing in round the window. Jake had his thick, red jumper on. Sophie hugged him – he was like a hot-water bottle.

"It has to," she nodded. "There's so much." She twisted round, looking up at the sky. It was dark grey and somehow it looked closer than usual, as if the weight of the snow was dragging it down. "And it's freezing," she added. "The frost hasn't melted since this morning. The snow will stick to it."

"A snowman," Jake murmured blissfully. "Will you build him with me, Sophie?" Jake pressed his nose right up against the glass. "I wish we had a sledge. We could go to the park. We could even go to school on a sledge!"

"School might be closed tomorrow," Sophie said hopefully. She liked school, but she certainly wouldn't say no to a day off – an extra bit of the weekend.

"No school!" Jake squeaked excitedly. He was only in Reception and he wasn't quite used to school yet. It seemed to involve an awful lot of sitting still on carpets and he wasn't very good at that, although he did like being with his friends.

"If you're lucky," Mum said, opening the sitting-room door and coming up behind them. "The weatherman on the radio said there's going to be lots of snow tonight." She leaned over to stare out of the window with them. "It's falling ever so fast."

There was a pattering scurry of paws over kitchen tiles and Sophie turned round, smiling. Biscuit had heard the door open and woken up at once. He practically skidded into the room, and let out a joyful, squeaky bark as he spotted Sophie and Jake.

"Look! Snow!" Jake squeaked back.

They sounded a lot like each other, Sophie thought. It wasn't all that surprising, since they were probably about the same age. Jake was four, and Biscuit was nearly six months old, which made him about four in dog years.

Biscuit was pawing happily at Jake's trousers and wagging his long, feathery, brown tail. Biscuit was a cocker spaniel cross — but no one was quite sure what he was crossed with. Whatever breed of dog it was, it had made his tail extra long and extra fluffy.

"Oh! Biscuit's never seen snow!" Sophie exclaimed. "I wonder what he'll think?" She got down, and picked Biscuit up round his fat middle. He loved being carried, which was lucky because Jake wanted to carry him everywhere.

Biscuit wriggled with excitement and licked Sophie all over — then he stopped licking and peered suspiciously over her shoulder at the window. It was getting dark, but he could still see that things looked odd. The garden almost seemed a different shape. He let out a questioning sort of yap, and Sophie stroked his ears.

"It's all right, Biscuit. It's snowing!" She giggled. "You might not like getting cold paws, though..."

"Well, I'm not taking him out for an evening walk in this," Mum said, shivering. "He'll have to wait until tomorrow for a proper walk." She eyed the swiftly falling snow again and frowned doubtfully. "Although it might be up to his nose by then..."

"So, is there school?" Sophie hovered hopefully next to her dad. She was wearing her pyjamas, dressing gown and slippers, and a scarf, and a woolly hat with ear flaps. Jake was standing beside her, dressed the same, except that he had his dinosaur

costume on instead of a dressing gown –
it had a great big padded tail, and it was
super-warm. Even though the heating was
on, and it wasn't really all that cold inside
the house, it was fun to wrap up.

The snow had still been falling when
they'd gone to bed last night. They'd
woken to find the morning sky clear and
sapphire blue, with the last of the moonlight
glimmering on a thick white coating of
snow.

The sun was up now and the snow was
sparkling. Sophie reckoned it had to be at
least fifteen centimetres deep. It had drifted
up against the garden fence and all Mum's
flower pots were covered. They were just
strange lumpy shapes, with the odd sad
little twig sticking out. The road in front

of the house was covered, too, with a dark grey double line of tyre tracks running down the middle.

It definitely didn't look like a day for school.

"No school," Dad said, with a smile. "It's just been announced."

"It's a snow day!" Sophie said delightedly, and Biscuit squirmed joyfully as she hugged him round the middle.

Dad grinned at her. "And the trains aren't running, either, so it's a snow day for me, too!"

"Are we going to build a snowman?" Jake hugged Dad round the legs excitedly.

"Yes. And I've got a surprise for you two." Dad smiled mysteriously.

"What? What?" Sophie begged, but Dad only shook his head, and his smile got bigger.

"Wait and see. Get dressed, and then we'd better have a big breakfast to help us keep warm."

"Can Biscuit be part of the surprise?" Sophie asked hopefully.

Dad looked thoughtful, then he nodded. "I don't see why not. He might like it…"

"Ohhhh!" Sophie groaned impatiently. Dad loved secrets. He could be so infuriating sometimes!

"Come on, Biscuit," Sophie coaxed, pulling gently on the puppy's lead.

Usually Biscuit leaped out of the front door with his tail whirling like a helicopter, but today he was completely flummoxed. Everything was wrong. There was no front path to race down, and no car to sniff at. Someone had taken away his front garden, and replaced it with a lot of odd white humpy things. And they smelled ... cold. Very cold. His nose twitched worriedly, and he pressed closer to Sophie's legs.

"I don't think he likes it," Sophie told Dad anxiously. "Look, he's got his tail between his legs."

"He's probably a bit upset," Mum said,

coming to rub Biscuit's nose. "He doesn't understand what's going on. But don't worry, he'll get used to it. Hey, Jake, careful!"

Jake was running round the front garden in his wellies, jumping and stomping and giggling at the snow. But there were things buried here and there – mostly sticks that Jake had brought home and abandoned – and it was hard to see them. Jake caught his foot and teetered, still giggling, and then collapsed face first in the snow.

"Oh no..." Dad muttered. "We haven't even got out of the garden and he's covered... Up you get, Jake."

Biscuit suddenly darted forward, nearly dragging his lead out of Sophie's hands. The snow was quite deep, banked up against the bushes, and Jake had almost disappeared.

As far as Biscuit could see, the nasty white stuff that had taken away his garden had now swallowed Jake, too. He wasn't having that. He launched himself across the garden, barking furiously, and tried to dig Jake out, snow flying madly under his burrowing paws.

Sophie chased after him, laughing. "It's OK, Biscuit! Jake's still there. Look, he's not even hurt – he likes it!"

Jake sat up, covered in snow but giggling as though it was the funniest thing that had ever happened. Mum and Dad brushed him off and Biscuit sniffed at him suspiciously, as if to make sure that Jake was all there – that the snow hadn't stolen any bits of him.

At least diving into the snow after Jake got Biscuit out of the doorway, Sophie thought. The little dog didn't look particularly keen on the snow – he kept lifting his paws up and staring at them – but he was in it at last.

"I think it's quite deep out there," she told Dad, looking at the street.

"I hope Biscuit can walk in it."

"I hope *Jake* can walk in it," Mum put in. "It could be over his wellies!"

"Aha!" Dad said smugly. "I may be able to help here."

"Is it the surprise?" Sophie demanded eagerly. "Please can you tell us now?"

Grinning at her, Dad went to open up the garage. Biscuit hopped through the snow and nosed hopefully round the doors. He never got to go in the garage, so he thought it must be full of the most exciting things...

"Uh-huh." Dad pushed Biscuit back gently as he reached in and pulled out...

"A sledge!" Sophie squealed, as Biscuit sniffed at the red plastic thoughtfully. "Oh! Is it ours?"

"Mm-hm. I saw it in the hardware shop last week, just when they were starting to talk about snow on the weather forecast, and I thought it might be fun. Try it out, Sophie," Dad said, putting the sledge down in front of her. "Jake can sit in front of you. I might not be able to pull you both all that far, but you can take turns after the first go. Ready?" Dad asked, giving the rope a little pull.

"Yes!"

"All right. Let's go!" Dad set off, pulling them out of the front garden and on to the pavement.

The sledge slipped over the snow, crunching it down with odd squeaky noises, and Sophie clutched tightly at Jake as they bumped along.

Mum followed behind, with Biscuit trailing on his lead, hopping doubtfully over the deep snow. He really wasn't sure about this white stuff. It was so cold, and it was wet as well, somehow. It was not good for the paws, not at all. His fur was all soggy, and his claws were tingling. And now they were leaving him behind! Jake and Sophie seemed to have forgotten all about him, giggling and squealing as they bounced along on the sledge. *They* weren't getting damp feet...

He scurried forward a little and took a flying leap. There – that was much better.

"Are you two wriggling?" Dad asked, turning back. "Be careful you don't tip the whole sledge over."

"Look, Dad!" Sophie called. "Look at Biscuit!"

"I *thought* it had got a bit harder to pull."
Dad rolled his eyes. "You lazy dog."

Biscuit was sitting triumphantly in
Jake's lap, staring down at the snowy road
as the sledge ran on. Maybe he could put up
with this white stuff after all…

THE LITTLE SNOW CAT

Tracey Corderoy

Once upon a time, in a faraway land, the sun was as yellow as buttercups. Big, fat bumblebees wriggled into flowers, rivers skipped over smooth rocks, and people grew sunflowers whose bright, nodding heads filled the sky!

Then the Ice Queen came — full of frosty magic. And with her came the snow, covering everything in a deep cold blanket of white. A whisper of fog crept from her lips, casting a spell over everyone, and the people of Bramble Down forgot all about sunshine and bees. It seemed that the snow had clothed their fields forever.

A hundred years passed and the Ice Queen lived on in her palace on the hill. And while the blizzards raged, she would never grow old. Bramble Down was in her icy grip...

Clara sat by the window. Bramble Down was growing dark, and snow was falling thicker than ever.

"Brrr!" she shivered, blowing on her hands. "My fingers are turning to icicles!"

"Sit here, then," called her grandmother from her chair by the fire as her needle went in and out. She sewed for a living, making warm woollen coats and hats.

But Clara liked her window seat too much to move. Since teatime she'd counted three plodding badgers and a hare wandering through the snowy garden.

Clara's grandmother got up and checked the soup on the stove. "Supper's ready!" she called. But Clara had spotted something much more important outside.

"A cat!" she beamed. "And it's pure white." Clara wanted a cat so much. "Grandma, please can it come inside?"

"But it belongs to someone else."

"I don't think it does!" said Clara quickly. She knew every cat in Bramble Down, but had never seen one as white as snow. "It could be my very own little snow cat!" She smiled. "Come and see!"

The cat was now sitting by the frozen pond, blinking up through the window at Clara. But when Clara's grandmother appeared at her side it shot off.

"Oh," Clara groaned. "Do you think it'll come back?"

"Perhaps," Grandmother nodded. "But certainly not before you've had your soup!"

All through supper Clara thought of the snow cat. That night she dreamed of it, too.

Then a noise downstairs woke her from her sleep. Throwing on her shawl, Clara tiptoed to see. And scratching at the window was…

"My snow cat!"

Clara opened
the window and
the cat hurried
in, out of the
howling blizzard.
"I'm Clara," she
whispered.

The little cat shivered.

"Here," said Clara. She took off her shawl, laid it on a chair and patted it. The cat leaped up and started padding about, purring softly.

Finally it sat down. Clara gently stroked it and began to tell it about her day...

"At school today my classroom was so chilly that we huddled together like penguins! And I'm knitting a bright purple scarf ... and my grandma is sewing a quilt!"

On and on Clara talked. It was great to have a new friend to talk to, even if it could only *purr* answers back!

After a while, the cat curled into a ball. But it had barely settled when footsteps up above made them both jump.

"Oh!" gasped Clara, checking the time.

"It's morning!"

With that, the snow cat shot to the window and started to paw the glass.

"You don't have to go," said Clara quickly. But the cat just pawed even more. Clara opened the window and the cat darted out.

"Do come back another time!" Clara called.

The cat did just that – the very next night, when Grandmother was fast asleep. And *this* time Clara gave it some fish she'd secretly squirrelled into her napkin at supper.

Once again, the cat was happy to stay. But only until early morning. Then it tapped on the window and Clara let it out.

"See you again when the moon comes out!" she whispered.

That night a howling gale rattled the windows but still the snow cat came.

"I've got a surprise for you." Clara smiled and took something out of her pocket. "A cloak to keep you warm!"

She'd sewn it after school that day. It was a deep red velvet, and as soft and warm as candlelight.

"Will you be my friend?" Clara asked. The little cat's ears pricked up.

"My *best* friend." Clara beamed. "Then you can stay all day!"

With that, there was a flash of light so bright that Clara had to shut her eyes. When she opened them again the cat had gone, and in its place sat a boy with white-blond hair, wearing strange, old-fashioned clothes.

"Who are *you*?" Clara gasped. *"And*

where's my cat?"

"I'm Gus," said the boy. "And I … was the cat."

"But how?"

"Well," said Gus, "about a hundred years ago, before I was a cat, I was a boy."

"You don't *look* a hundred," Clara frowned.

"The Ice Queen put a spell on me," Gus explained, "and turned me into a cat. As long as I've been under her magic, I've never grown old."

"The Ice Queen did *that*?" Clara gasped, and Gus gave a small nod.

"Before *she* came, everything was good," he said. "I played outside all the time, and Bramble Down was full of flowers."

"Flowers?" repeated Clara. "What are those?"

Gus tried to describe the way everything used to be, but it was really hard.

"Maybe you could *draw* it instead," suggested Clara.

She hurried to the dresser and found some paper and pencils.

The picture Gus drew was of the loveliest place Clara had ever seen. The things called flowers were so pretty!

"These stripey things are *bees*," Gus explained.

Next he drew children in his picture, playing and laughing outside. "And that yellow ball in the sky is the *sun!*" Gus smiled.

"So why," said Clara, now brimming with questions, "did the Ice Queen turn you into a cat?"

Gus's bright smile disappeared at once.

"The day she came to Bramble Down," replied Gus, "I'd gone off searching for fossils. But I got a bit lost and ended up miles away. When I finally found my way home, everything in Bramble Down had changed."

"Changed?" said Clara.

"There was snow everywhere, the wind was howling and the Ice Queen had appeared with her palace of ice on the hill. When I asked where the sun had gone, no one had a clue what I was talking about. It was like their memories had been clouded by a thick, white fog."

"So what happened next?" Clara asked.

"I worked out that the Ice Queen had brought the blizzards and wiped everyone's memories!" said Gus. "All except mine, because I'd been away. So I marched to her palace and told her she had to go."

Clara gasped. "But she didn't."

"No – she just got really angry," replied Gus, "and cast a spell that turned me into a cat. That way, I couldn't talk about sunshine, and it would carry on snowing forever. She kept me locked in her chilly cellar."

"So how did you escape?" Clara cried.

"I dug a tunnel," Gus said proudly. "Claws are good at cutting through ice! Every night, I crept out of the palace, and searched for the right person to help me break the spell. Then every morning I had to race back to the palace so the Ice Queen wouldn't realize that I had found a way out. Night after night I looked for someone to help me, but nobody could break the spell. Until I found you!"

"But what did *I* do?" Clara looked puzzled.

"You were *kind* to me – three nights in a row," smiled Gus. "You shared your shawl, your food and your friendship. So your warm heart broke the spell!"

Clara picked up the picture Gus had drawn.

"And what about outside?" she asked. "Now we've broken the Ice Queen's spell on *you*, can we turn everything else back, too?"

Gus shrugged. "The Ice Queen told me that as long as people knew nothing of sunshine, the blizzards would never stop."

"But," Clara cried, "you just told me! So now *I* know about sunshine." They looked through the window, but snow was still tumbling down.

"Maybe if we tell *more* people?" said Clara. "Or – even better – *show* them!"

She asked if Gus could draw his picture bigger.

"As big as a flag," she said. "Then we'll hold it up in the village square so that *everyone* can see it!"

The problem was, bigger paper would be torn by the wind and soaked by the swirling snow. So they searched for something stronger instead.

Finally, Clara found a bundle of white fabric at the bottom of her grandmother's sewing box.

"That looks good," nodded Gus, "except pencils won't show up on it."

"We'll just have to *sew* your picture instead, then!" grinned Clara.

They got to work. They had to move fast, in case the Ice Queen realized her cat was missing. If she did, she would come to look for him, angrier than a blizzard.

On and on and on they stitched – until the black night sky began to turn grey. At last, Clara snipped the final thread.

"Oh!" She smiled. Their tapestry was *beautiful*, full of bright colours and completely unlike the outside world that Clara had always known. But would it be able to bring back the sunshine again?

Clara called up to her grandmother, telling her to come to the village square – now! Then she found some coats for her and Gus, and they trudged off through the snow, knocking on every door they passed on the way.

Bleary-eyed villagers peeped out in their nightclothes.

"We've got something to show you," Clara called. "Follow us!"

The village square was deep with snow as people, now in pyjamas *and* coats, watched Clara and the strange boy unroll a huge piece of fabric. But what could they have to show that was so important?

The wind was whipping up into a gale. Gus shuddered and wondered whether the Ice Queen had discovered that her little snow cat was missing.

As they held up the tapestry, Clara's grandmother appeared.

"Clara! What's that you've got there?"

"It's how Bramble Down *used* to be!" Clara called to everyone.

"Sunshine, flowers, bees…" Clara chanted.

"Grass, trees, ladybirds…" added Gus.

As they chanted on, to the crowd's great surprise, the falling snow began to grow lighter. Big flakes turned to smaller flakes. Then smaller flakes turned to tiny ones that dissolved before their eyes.

The last snowflake melted, and as it did, a horrified wail echoed through the air…

"Nooooo!"

The villagers recognized the Ice Queen's voice. But she sounded so different. Quite desperate! Could it have something to do with Clara and the boy?

Now Clara felt the tapestry in her hands was growing warm. Then suddenly it transformed into a whirl of bright petals, hiding everything from sight!

Like confetti, they fluttered gently to the ground, and…

"Look!" gasped the crowd. "What *is* it?"

Instead of the snow, there was now soft green grass, and there were flowers everywhere! Bees buzzed through the turquoise sky, and a big yellow sun shone down on them all.

"We did it!" cheered Gus.

Where the ice palace had once towered, now a forest of sunflowers nodded brightly.

Gus and Clara raced to them through buttercups as yellow as the sun. There was no sign of the Ice Queen now, but standing before the sunflowers was a beautiful blossom tree, covered in soft, white petals!

Things changed in Bramble Down after that. Everyone kept their doors open wide to let in the golden sunshine, and giggling children raced through jungles of grass!

It still snowed, but only at Christmas. And then it was soft, fluffy snow. Snow that you could build snowmen with. Though

Clara and Gus preferred to build snow *cats* instead!

HO! HO! HO!

Jeanne Willis

It was Christmas Eve. It had been snowing hard all day. The fields were white, the wind whistled through the woods and the duck pond was frozen. The farmer was busy chopping wood in the yard, so he didn't feel the cold.

Nor did the farmer's wife. She was in the farmhouse by the hot stove, baking mince pies, boiling plum puddings and making cakes. As for the farmer's daughter, she was toasting her toes by a roaring fire with the farm cat curled up on her lap.

The icy weather didn't bother them at all. It didn't bother the sheep, either – they had fleecy, snowproof coats. The calves and the lambs were in the barn, tucked up in the hay. The donkey had a blanket, the chicks slept under the hen's fluffy feathers and it was lovely weather for robins.

But Piglet was freezing. He had no fur, no feathers and no fire to keep him warm.

It was his first winter – the first time he'd ever seen the snow. It should have been fun, but it wasn't. He had never felt so cold in all his life. More than anything, he wanted to have a happy Christmas, so rather than sit there shivering, he decided to do something about it.

Braving the weather, the plucky piglet

trotted across the farmyard on his bare feet, slipping and sliding on the ice.

"Brrr… I'm frozen from my head to my hooves," he said. "I need something to wear."

Just then, he spotted a small pair of red trousers hanging from the washing line. They belonged to the farmer's son. He brushed the icicles off and put the trousers on.

"That's better," he said. "My tail is nice and warm now, but my trotters have frostbite. If only I had some shoes, I shouldn't mind the snow in the slightest."

He wandered past the farmhouse and there, on the front step, was a pair of black boots. They belonged to the farmer's daughter. Piglet sat down and put them on his back feet. They were a bit big, but that didn't put him off. He stuffed the toes with straw.

"That's better. They fit perfectly now," he said, marching up and down on two legs. "I've got toasty trotters but my sh-sh-shoulders are shivering."

He jumped up and down to try and warm up, but it was impossible in wellingtons.

"If only I had a coat," he said, stomping along the path.

As he came to the stables, he saw a bright red jacket with a furry hood hanging on a hook. It belonged to the stable girl. Piglet stopped and tried it on. It was a bit tight round the tummy, but after a struggle, he pulled the zip all the way up to his chin and put the hood on. It was so big, it fell right over his snout, but Piglet was pleased.

"That's better," he said. "My shoulders and ears and snout are snug."

But a bitter wind was blowing and there were no toggles on the hood to tie it tight.

"There's a terrible draught round my neck," said Piglet. "What I need is a scarf."

He knew he'd seen one somewhere on the farm. He looked in the cowshed, but it wasn't there. He looked in the goat pen, but it wasn't there. It wasn't in the tractor shed, either.

"Never mind," said Piglet. "I'll just have to do without it."

Then suddenly, he remembered. He climbed over the stile and hurried down the lane. He ran across the cabbage field as fast as he could towards the scarecrow. It was wearing a tatty hat, a tartan shirt and torn trousers but round its neck was a fluffy white scarf that used to belong to the farmer's wife.

Piglet took the scarf from the scarecrow and wrapped it round his neck three times. "I promise to bring it back," he said.

Piglet plodded back across the field and down the lane. "That's better," he said. "My neck is lovely and warm in this scarf. Now I can have fun! I will make a snowman."

Piglet gathered snow from the snowdrift by the stile. He made a big snowball for the body and a little snowball for the head. He picked velvety black sloe berries to make its eyes and shiny red holly berries to make a smile. He added some twigs for arms and pebbles for buttons then stood back to admire his handiwork. It was a fine snowman but Piglet's front trotters were so cold from playing with the snow, they had gone numb.

"I need some gloves," he said. "Never mind, maybe I'll get some for Christmas."

He climbed over the stile and made

his way back to the farmyard, but on the way, he saw something stuck in a bush. At first he thought it was sheep's wool – but it wasn't. It was a pair of mittens with silver bells sewn to the cuffs! When he shook the snow off, they jingled.

"The little girl who lived down the lane must have lost them," said Piglet. "I'm sure she won't mind if I borrow them." He put the mittens on. "That's much better. *All* of me is lovely and warm now," he said. "I'm tingling, jingling and all dressed for winter… But oh, dear! My house is so bleak, it's colder inside than it is outside."

Just then, he saw smoke coming from the farmhouse chimney and had an idea.

"What I need is some wood to make a fire," said Piglet.

He went to the grain store and found a sack of corn. He tipped out all the corn and hurried to the place where the farmer chopped logs. There was lots of timber left, so he gathered it up, filled his sack to the brim and tied the top.

"Now I will be able to eat my Christmas dinner in comfort," he said.

It was getting dark. The stars were out and the snow was still falling. In the distance, he could hear the church bells chime.

"Time to go home," said Piglet.

He picked up the sack of wood, slung it over his shoulder and went on his way. But the snow was so deep and the sack was so heavy, he had to keep stopping.

"I'm puffed out," said Piglet. "I wish I had something to carry me home."

The Christmas Fairy must have heard him, for his wish came true. As Piglet staggered round the corner, he saw something red and gold and shiny sticking out of the snow among the fir trees. It was a beautiful, brightly painted sledge. It belonged to the shepherd's boy – Piglet had seen him racing it down the hill, past the pig pen, to give the lambs their breakfast in the barn.

Piglet could hardly believe his luck. He put his bulging sack of wood in the back of the sledge and sat on the seat. The shepherd's boy wouldn't mind if he borrowed it – he was very fond of pigs.

"I'll bring it back tomorrow," promised Piglet.

He held on to the reins tightly and whooshed down the hill with his hood over his face and his fluffy scarf trailing like an old man's beard.

As he flew towards the barn, the sound of the bells jingling on his mittens woke a little lamb. She ran over to the window and bleated in surprise. "Look!" she cried.

The donkey and the calf ran over to see what all the fuss was about.

"Ooh… Is it really *him*?" squealed the calf.

Dashing past in a sleigh was a figure

dressed from head to toe in red, with a long, snowy beard and a sack full of ... presents?

"It's Father Christmas!" said the lamb. "Who else could it be? I told you he would come if we were good!"

Just then, they heard the sound of jolly laughter coming from above. "Ho! Ho! Ho!" it went. "Ho! Ho! Ho!"

They gazed up in wonder at the big sleigh landing on the farmhouse roof. Then they gazed down in amazement at the little sleigh flying over the hill towards the pig pen.

"We must have been very, very good!" said Donkey. "There are *two* Father Christmases!"

The animals could hardly believe their eyes. Only Piglet knew the truth.

As for the real Father Christmas, he didn't know what to believe!

But you do, don't you?

THE DOG SLED

Michelle Misra

Maska raised an eyebrow and shifted his weight from one paw to the other as he waited. His ears twitched and his tail curled over his back.

"Woof, woof, woof!" He barked impatiently, wondering what his new partner in the dog-sled team would be like now that Luna had been retired.

Although Maska was a husky and had a fluffy layer of fur under his thick topcoat, the snow was falling heavily and he was starting to feel cold. He wanted the race to begin. They were competing in an Alaskan dog-sled race that would take over ten days, crossing a thousand miles of ice and four mountain ranges, passing frozen lakes and snowy rivers. There would be dangers, too – not least the challenges from wolves and moose – but Maska was used to that. He was ten years old and had been competing in the race for most of his life with the man who drove the sled – his musher – and thirteen other dogs. With his short, muscular body and strong nose for scent, he was the perfect leader and loved nothing better than running in harness, and hearing the buzz of the crowd.

Mush, Mush, Mush!

The other dogs shuffled in the reins.

Anouk and Dakota – the first of the two sets of point dogs – were directly behind him. Then there were two sets of swing dogs, who took the weight of the curve and two sets of wheel dogs at the back near the sled where the musher stood. The wheel dogs would have to pull the hardest if the sled got stuck in snow but Maska's job, as team leader, was definitely the most important. He had to watch out for danger and control the team.

"What's keeping them?" Dakota whined, his breath forming little clouds of smoke on the cold air.

"Not sure," Maska growled. He was starting to feel a bit grumpy, what with all the waiting. But Maska wasn't one to complain. His name meant big and strong so he wouldn't make a fuss.

Ah, here they were at last. He could see his musher approaching now, wearing a padded bearskin coat and earflap hat. But who was that with him? Maska's blue eyes narrowed as he took in the little Alaskan husky who was jumping excitedly around his master's feet, yapping and yelping.

Maska let out a warning growl.

"Meet your new partner, Maska," said the musher. "He's called Apache."

"*Apache?*" Maska growled again. What kind of a name was that? He'd expected his new partner to be an older dog, too, but this young pup couldn't be more than a year or two old.

"Woof, woof, woof!" the new dog called out cheerfully.

Maska's eyes narrowed. They'd tried to pair him with other sled dogs in the past, but it had never worked. Luna had been perfect because he'd been happy to let Maska lead, but this young pup looked fairly self-assured. And now his musher was putting Apache into four new booties before tying him into the harness next to Maska.

"Woof, woof, woof!" the new dog barked again.

"All right, that's enough, Apache," the musher said. "Settle down."

As the musher turned away, the new dog turned to Maska. "Hi there, boss."

"Ugh." Maska turned away and ignored him, looking out over the ice-swept landscape to where the other sleds had already congregated and crowds of people lined the ropes.

"So what's this like? This race?" Apache woofed as the musher guided them into position. But there wasn't time to talk now.

"Hike!" the musher cried. The flag went down and they were off! The sled whistled its way down the wide path to the sound of clapping and cheering. It didn't take long before the town was left far behind, a speck in the distance, and the dog sleds were out in the open spaces. The other sleds started to slow down and spread out, and the musher eased them into a gentler pace.

"So how long have you been doing this trip, partner?" Apache panted to Maska, bouncing about in the reins.

"Partner?" Maska muttered under his breath. Still, to be fair, the young pup didn't know what he was saying and he seemed to be a hard worker.

"Eight years," he panted back.

"Eight years? Quite an expert," Apache called. "Talking of expert, I've got a joke for you. What do you call the place where sled dogs are trained? The *mushroom*. Mush? Get it?"

Maska let out an impatient growl. This young pup wasn't taking the race any way near seriously enough. Apache was already starting to get on his nerves and they had another nine days to get through together.

As they passed tree-lined slopes, the wind picked up, turning the falling flakes into a blizzard.

Maska tuned out and tried to focus on leading the pack. Now they were speeding along, cruising through the landscape and into the biting wind. The path had been cut in advance of the race and snow was banked up on each side as they scurried along.

"*Mush, mush, mush,*" the musher called, pushing them faster into a running gait.

Beside him, Apache was still telling jokes, calling out to the other dogs. Past lakes and crossing over fields, they raced onwards and Maska started to feel tired. His legs weren't as young as they used to be. He thought that there could only be another hour of running tonight before they'd reach the checkpoint and settle down and rest, though.

Sure enough, they rounded the corner and Maska saw the orange lights in the distance that meant they were nearly there. At last!

"Whoa!" the musher cried.

They slowed the turn and came into the camp. One by one, the musher took the dogs off the lead ropes and led them over to a bed of straw.

The dogs leaped happily at their food and lapped thirstily at the water that had been put out for them. Maska was relieved when the booties were finally taken from his feet and he could rest. He joined the other dogs on the straw bedding and licked his paws, nipping and biting them to ease the ache within.

"You all right?"

Maska turned to see the pup beside him again. "Why wouldn't I be?" he growled.

"I just... It's just that... Oh, it's nothing..."

"No, go on," Maska said, his eyes

narrowing.

"Well," Apache started. "I couldn't help but notice… I mean, you seemed tired near the end."

Maska snarled.

"I didn't mean any harm by it," Apache whimpered.

Maska felt guilty. He knew that Apache hadn't really meant it unkindly and that the pup had had to take a fair amount of the weight that day – more than he should have.

As the huskies settled down into their warm bedding for the night, Maska could hear the young pup entertaining the other dogs with more jokes. Would he never stop talking?

"*Mush, mush, mush...* Get up! Hurry ... hurry ... hurry..."

It was still dark the next morning when the huskies woke and were put into their harnesses. The musher hooked them up in pairs and attached the ropes.

"How are you feeling this morning, boss?" Apache called cheerily to Maska.

"Not so bad," the older husky snuffled back, although it wasn't exactly true. It had been a long day yesterday and he was pretty stiff in his legs.

"You look tired," Apache said.

"I'm fine," snapped Maska.

Apache shrugged his shoulders and took his place next to Maska and soon they were off again. As they left the encampment, lights sprang up all around.

The musher was carrying a torch in one hand to see the way and the dogs had little reflectors on them. They raced gently at first but soon they were running faster and faster, the wind whipping past them and flurries of snow nearly blinding them.

Maska started to slow down. His muscles were aching from the day before. He willed himself on. But next to him, he could feel Apache struggling under the weight of the sled, which meant that they weren't running at an even pace. The sled was all akimbo and if he wasn't careful, they would turn it over.

One... two... three... They were getting faster and faster and now they were heading for a corner. Maska couldn't keep up. If he didn't take his share of the weight, the sled would topple.

"Look out!" Apache howled.

Something flashed in front of them! A big, brown creature with forked antlers and heavy shoulders. A moose!

Quick as a flash, Apache reacted. He pulled the sled out of the way of the moose and then steered it back into a straight line, just in time for Maska to catch up as they took the weight of the corner. Phew! They had narrowly avoided a collision.

As the more experienced dog, Maska knew that he should have been the one to do that, but he'd been so tired that he hadn't been concentrating. If it hadn't been for Apache's quick thinking – warning the others and steering the sled – they would have collided with the moose.

The animal shot off into the distance and the sled drew to a halt. The musher walked round to the front of the sled to check on all the dogs.

"I think we had a lucky escape there, boys, thanks to our top dogs up front." He patted Maska and Apache on their heads.

Maska looked over at
Apache, expecting him
to say something to
the other dogs, but
he stayed quiet.

"Thank you,
Apache," Maska
finally muttered
under his breath to the pup, as they started
on their way again. "You saved the day."

"Think nothing of it," Apache said. "Isn't
that what a team's for?"

As the snow settled on the heads of the
two dogs, Maska took a deep breath. "OK.
Partners," he breathed.

"Partners." Apache grinned back. "Now,
come on. Haven't we got a race to run?"

HIGGY'S
WINTER
WONDERLAND

MICHAEL BROAD

Higgy the hedgehog and his woodland friends were heading home from a day of play, running and laughing. The late autumn sunset glowed pink and orange through the trees. Their first winter was on its way and the young animals were excited. They kicked fallen leaves and dashed along bare branches, enjoying the seasonal changes in Old Oak Wood and looking forward to those still to come.

"I can't wait to see the winter snow," said

Rilly the squirrel, waving his paws. "My mum said Jack Frost shakes snowflakes from the clouds and makes everything sparkle."

"My dad says Jack Frost draws patterns with a magic quill," added Gabby the rabbit. She plucked a twig and swished it about artistically. "He covers the whole wood with frosty flowers and makes everything beautiful."

"I heard that Jack Frost is a magical spirit. That he creates everything in one night and gives it a special name," said Betty the badger. Everyone slowed down as she lowered her voice to a whisper. "It's called *the Winter Wonderland.*"

"WOW!" gasped Rilly and Gabby.

"Who's Jack Frost?" asked Higgy,

shuffling through the leaves and struggling to keep up with his friends. The little hedgehog was feeling left out of the conversation. Why hadn't his mum told *him* anything about this magical spirit or the Winter Wonderland?

"No one really knows who or what Jack Frost is because no one has ever seen him," replied Betty, considering the question carefully. "But he must be a clever spirit to create the Winter Wonderland all by himself, so I imagine he's probably a badger."

"But he must also be creative," added Gabby, casually sketching out a daisy in the ground with her twig. "Which makes me think that he's definitely a rabbit."

"Cleverness and creativity would be no

use without speed," said Rilly. He dashed up the nearest tree and shot back down again in no time at all. "So of all the woodland animals, Jack Frost is most likely to be a squirrel."

"Could he be a hedgehog?" Higgy asked hopefully.

The other animals looked at him and giggled.

"I don't think so," said Rilly. "Hedgehogs are not very fast."

"They do have quills," said Gabby, hopping around Higgy to get a better look at his coat of tiny spines. "But I don't see how one could draw nice flowers with them."

"You're all forgetting the most important thing," said Betty. The badger was a little older than her friends and also very knowledgeable. "Hedgehogs *hibernate* during the winter, so they would be no good at all."

"What does 'hibernate' mean?" asked Higgy.

"Has your mum been giving you extra food?" Betty asked.

Higgy rested his paws on his large, round belly and nodded.

"And have you felt more sleepy than usual?"

Higgy was about to answer "yes", but then yawned loudly instead.

"Hibernating animals eat as much food as they can before the cold weather comes," explained Betty. "And then they sleep all winter and don't wake up again until the warm weather returns in the spring."

"Oh," sighed Higgy. He suddenly realized that his mum *had* told him all about hibernation, but he had thought she meant they were going on holiday. That explained why his mum hadn't spoken of Jack Frost or the Winter Wonderland.

The four friends continued to ponder the mystery of Jack Frost until they reached the old oak tree where they lived. Betty's home was in the underground badger tunnels. Gabby's rabbit hole was deep below the trunk. Rilly's cosy squirrel hollow was at the top of the tree, and Higgy's hedgehog den was at the bottom, between the roots.

"I've had a brilliant idea!" exclaimed Betty, before they went their separate ways. "I think we should make a pact to find Jack Frost this winter!"

"How?" asked Rilly and Gabby.

"By patrolling during the day and keeping watch through the night," said Betty. "We can take it in turns so someone is always on the lookout and then we'll all get to see who creates the Winter Wonderland!"

"Not *all* of us," sighed Higgy, realizing that he would miss out on all the fun. "I'll be fast asleep and snoring while you all have an adventure without me."

"I wish you could join us," said Rilly.

"It won't be the same without you," added Gabby.

"We'll tell you all about it in the spring," said Betty. "I promise."

As the days grew colder and the evenings darkened, Higgy spent more time with his mum, preparing for their long winter sleep. They swept out the den and changed the bedding, and then gathered all the food they could find for one last meal. Higgy's mum tried to keep his spirits up. She knew that the little hedgehog wanted to stay awake with his friends, especially when Gabby, Rilly and Betty came to say goodbye.

Before they left, Higgy wanted to hear all about his friends' plans to look for Jack Frost. So they took him to see the hide they had built, from which they planned to watch over the wood in secret.

"We made it from willow to keep out the draughts," said Gabby, patting the tightly woven dome. "And stuck twigs in for camouflage so the Jack Frost *rabbit* won't see it."

"She means the Jack Frost *squirrel*," laughed Rilly, climbing into the hide and peeping through a tiny window near the top. "And *this* is where we'll watch him create the Winter Wonderland."

"Don't pay any attention to those two," said Betty, as they each gave Higgy a farewell hug. "Just have a good hibernation and we'll tell you all about the Jack Frost *badger* when you wake in the spring."

Higgy returned home and snuggled down with his mum for his first hibernation. He had hoped to stay up a little longer, just in case Jack Frost arrived early. But the bedding was so warm and his belly was so full that he felt more sleepy than ever before. His mum sang a gentle lullaby as Higgy closed his eyes, and the little hedgehog made a single wish before he fell asleep.

"Please let me wake to see the Winter Wonderland," he whispered.

Higgy then slept and dreamed of sparkling snow and frosty flowers, and all the things his friends had told him about the Winter Wonderland. He couldn't see Jack Frost in his dream, but he thought he heard someone calling his name – it travelled on the chill wind that whistled through the trees. Higgy was sure the voice belonged to Jack Frost, and it sounded so real that he stirred in his den until his eyes fluttered open in the darkness.

The little hedgehog crept away from his sleeping mother until he reached the opening of their den, squinting at the light coming from outside. Higgy thought it must be daytime, but then he saw flakes of white glowing in the moonlight on the roots of the oak tree and stepped out into the bright snowy night.

The ground was covered with a soft quilt of snow and giant flakes swirled around him. The snow made sloping drifts against tree trunks and coated bare branches, making the whole wood look as though it was dressed in white lace. The Winter Wonderland was well under way and, once again, the little hedgehog heard someone calling his name.

Higgy ran through the wood in search of the mysterious caller, and enjoyed the sensation of snow beneath his paws. Up ahead he saw a large snowdrift. On top he could make out a silhouette. It was round and spiny just like him.

"Jack Frost," he whispered, hurrying up the mound. "Could he really be a—"

Just as the little hedgehog climbed to the top of the drift, the bristly shape turned round and stood up to his full height. Below the crown of sparkling spines was the face of a human boy. The boy was tall and thin with pale skin, and he crouched down to smile at Higgy.

"You came," the boy said kindly.

"Jack Frost?" said Higgy. "I thought you were..."

"A hedgehog?" Jack chuckled, ruffling the

spiky hair that sprang from his head like crisp white icicles. "I'm not one myself, but I could never create the Winter Wonderland without my little helpers."

Higgy looked around and saw furry white hedgehogs peering out at him from the drifts, almost invisible against the snow. The animals were all creamy white because their brown quills were no longer on their backs but hovering in the air above them! Higgy watched wide-eyed as the hedgehogs waved their paws and sent the quills flying off around the trees, conducting them here and there in a magical dance, their points etching frosty flowers throughout Old Oak Wood.

"Hedgehogs all across the land are drawing their amazing patterns," Jack Frost stated proudly. "Only the cleverest, fastest and most creative hedgehogs can make the Winter Wonderland, and that's why I called out to you," he smiled.

"Wow!" said Higgy.

Higgy quickly learned all the secrets of the hedgehogs and their midwinter magic, and drew beautiful patterns with his own little spines. He etched feathered vines on tree trunks and spiky stars on frozen puddles, and even made a collection of frosty flowers to give to his mother. When the work was done, Higgy played in the Winter Wonderland with Jack Frost and the other lucky helpers until just before sunrise, when the sleepy hedgehogs headed back to their dens.

On the way home, Higgy stopped at his friends' willow hide and peeped in through the window. Gabby, Rilly and Betty were all fast asleep and snoring loudly, unaware of the magic that had happened outside. Higgy did not want to wake them and was very tired himself. So he etched simple outlines of a rabbit, a squirrel and a badger where he was sure they would see them. Then Higgy whispered a promise to tell his friends all about his magical adventure when he saw them again in the spring.

Have you read…

A Collection of Adorable Animal Stories

MOONLIGHT

Magic

Illustrated by
Alison Edgson

WINTER Magic

A Spellbinding Collection of Christmas Animal Tales

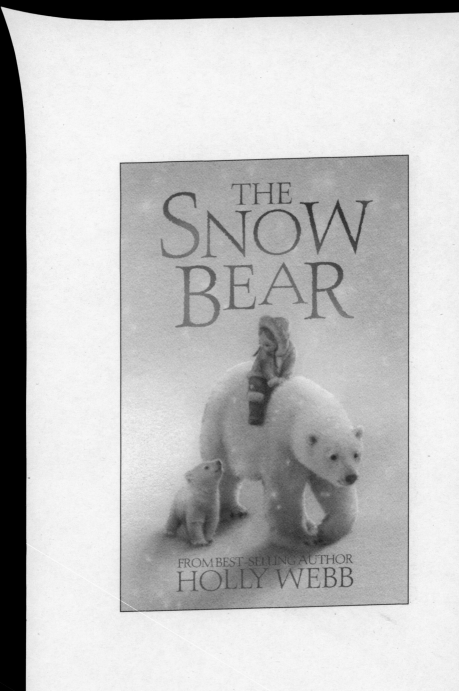

THE SNOW BEAR

FROM BEST-SELLING AUTHOR
HOLLY WEBB

The
Reindeer
Girl

From best-selling author
Holly Webb

The
Storm
Leopards

FROM BEST-SELLING AUTHOR
HOLLY WEBB

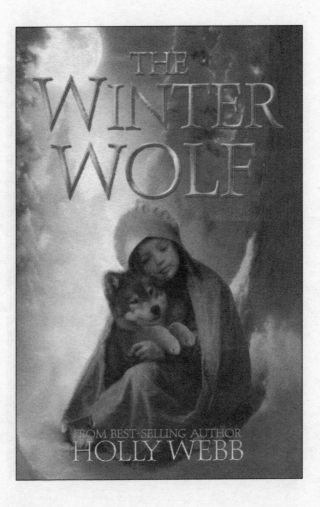

THE
WINTER
WOLF

FROM BEST-SELLING AUTHOR
HOLLY WEBB

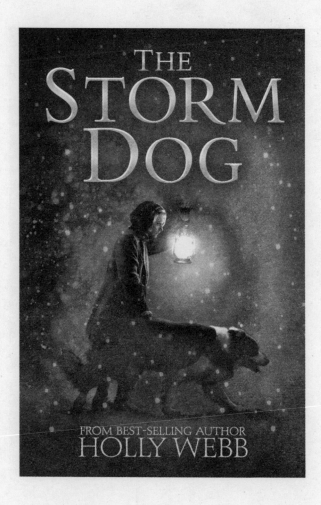

THE STORM DOG

FROM BEST-SELLING AUTHOR
HOLLY WEBB